My Teacher Is a Martian!

Left without a teacher, our class was going crazy. Paper airplanes sailed through the air. A spitball hit me in the face.

"What happened in the office?" Nicho yelled. "Fargo's not coming back, is she?"

"She freaked out," I told Nicho. "Now Dr. Drucker's calling in some guy from Mars."

You could hear a pin drop. Everyone was staring at me.

"That's what Drucker said." I gulped. Then I said it again in case they hadn't heard me the first time.

"We're going to have a substitute teacher from Mars."

THE SUBSTITUTE TEACHER FROM

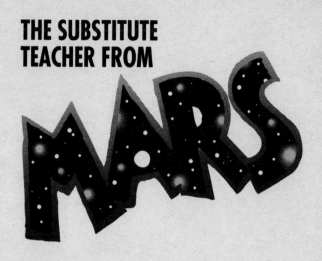

by

Elaine Moore

Troll Associates

Library of Congress Cataloging-in-Publication Data

Moore, Elaine.
  The substitute teacher from Mars / by Elaine Moore.
      p.   cm.
  Summary: The students of Mrs. Meriweather's sixth grade class are
champions at getting rid of substitute teachers until they come up
against the unusual Mr. Marrs.
  ISBN 0-8167-3283-3 (pbk.)
  [1. Schools—Fiction.   2. Substitute teachers—Fiction.]
I. Title.
PZ7.M7832Su   1994
[Fic]—dc20   93-37527

A TROLL BOOK, published by Troll Associates, Inc.

To all my buddies (students, staff, and subs)
at Swift Creek Elementary.

CHAPTER 1

"Psst, Donatelli! Dead Bug at two o'clock. Got it?"

That's Nicho. Nicho sits across from me. He's trying to get me—Jerry Donatelli—and the rest of our sixth-grade class in trouble.

If I stay hunched over and keep drawing, Nicho will think I don't hear him.

Fortunately, Mrs. Fargo doesn't hear him. She's too busy writing our math assignment on the chalkboard.

It's 1:45. Somehow I have to last until 1:55. That's when I'll raise my hand and ask to be excused. I'll say I have to go the nurse's office to take my allergy medicine. I don't really have to take my allergy medicine at 1:55. It comes in a bottle and I can take it any time. I can also take it any day I please, depending on whether or not my nose is stuffed up, but Mrs. Fargo is a substitute teacher and she won't know that.

"Psst, Kelly." Nicho's at it again. "Dead Bug at two o'clock. Be ready."

Today is Friday. Mrs. Fargo is the fourth substitute teacher we've had this week. She doesn't stand a chance.

"Psst, Sharon . . . "

Sharon sits on the other side of Nicho and one row up from me. When Nicho signals Sharon, it's hard to keep my head down. Every time Sharon looks remotely in my direction, my ears start to burn and I feel a stupid grin spread across my face.

1:50.

Behind me, a book dropped. *Bang!* A girl giggled. You could feel tension in the air. Everyone was waiting for two o'clock.

At two o'clock, Nicho would cup his hands around his mouth.

"Dead Bug!" he'd shout.

All the kids would fall out of their chairs, even the girls. Rolling over on their backs, they'd paw at the air with their arms and kick their legs like a bunch of dead bugs.

Our class does Dead Bug every day we have a substitute teacher.

It's part of Nicho's master plan. According to Nicho, if we go through twenty-five subs before our regular teacher, Mrs. Meriweather, returns from maternity leave, our class will make the *Guinness*

Book of World Records.

"Think of it this way," Nicho announced in the cafeteria. "Our names will be in the same book with the person who swallowed ninety-nine goldfish and the guy who can twist his ankles over his shoulders like a pretzel."

We have pulled a bunch of tricks. So far, there's been a rubber worm and spider, a whoopie cushion, and plastic throw-up. Nicho smeared honey on one sub's chair and then the whole class switched seats after recess so the sub couldn't tell who was who. But of every stunt our class pulls, Dead Bug is the best. Dead Bug really shakes up a sub.

I only took part in Dead Bug once and that was only because I wanted to find out what it would feel like to be a dead bug. It felt even stupider than my stupid grin.

Plus, in addition to feeling stupid, I felt kind of sorry for the substitute when she went bonkers and ran screaming down the hall. I kept thinking that my mom is a teacher. What if a bunch of kids played Dead Bug on her?

Lucky for me, Mrs. Fargo put the chalk down when the book dropped. Then she turned around to face the class. Judging by her expression, she knew something was about to happen. She just didn't know what or when.

Quickly, I shot my hand up in the air.

Mrs. Fargo frowned. Did she think I was part of whatever bad thing was about to happen?

"Yes?"

"May I be excused to go to the nurse's office? I have to take my allergy medicine."

"Certainly. Here's a pass."

By two o'clock, I'd taken my medicine and was sitting on the couch in the main office, right outside the nurse's office. It's a rule. After I take my medicine, I have to wait fifteen minutes before returning to my classroom, just in case I have a bad reaction or something. Since our school nurse never knows when a really sick kid might show up, she lets me hang out in the office.

Except for when my dad had cancer, my mom's always been pretty easygoing about medical stuff. But at school, they have to be extra-careful. If something bad happens to a kid, they might get sued or something. I know because I read about it in the newspaper.

Reading newspapers is one of my favorite things to do. You would be surprised at the neat stuff you can find in the paper. Like how some parents will sue a school the instant something bad happens to their kid. It's a thing grownups do. Even if the kid is a trouble-maker, parents will still sue a school.

So there I was, plopped on the couch in the main office, calmly minding my manners and doing my best to keep Bigelow Springs Elementary from being sued when the office door was practically ripped off its hinges and Mrs. Fargo came bursting inside.

"DR. DRUCKER!"

She screamed so loud for the principal, I almost

fell off the couch.

Lucky for the school, Mrs. Fargo didn't burst my eardrums.

But I don't think Mrs. Fargo was thinking much about my eardrums, because before I could scoot safely out of her way, she stuck her red fingernail dangerously close to my nose.

"Don't think I don't recognize you," she hollered. "You're one of them!"

Our substitute teacher was having a rabies fit in the main office.

The next thing I knew, Mrs. Fargo was staggering past the little room where first graders go to throw up and heading into the principal's office.

Wow.

I leaned forward on the couch cushions. I didn't want Mrs. Fargo to accuse me of being part of something I had just taken a spoonful of nasty-tasting medicine to avoid.

I didn't want Dr. Drucker to call my mom and make her think she wasn't doing a good job raising two boys without having a husband around. I didn't want her to worry that she had an eleven-year-old juvenile delinquent for a son.

I also didn't want Dr. Drucker to ask me what was going on in my classroom. No way did I want to tell him about Nicho's plan to get us in the *Guinness Book of World Records*. Forget that Nicho wasn't my friend. Forget that I didn't have any friends and the kids thought I was a nerd. I wasn't a rat fink.

Maybe I ought to leave, I thought. But then how would I find out what was happening with Mrs. Fargo and Dr. Drucker?

Just then a door slammed and Dr. Drucker stormed out of his office.

He looked at me and right away told the secretary, "Get Superintendent Brady on the phone."

Uh-oh. I couldn't leave now.

I tried making a big show of checking my watch against the clock on the wall and looking at my watch again, just in case someone thought I was hanging around to find out what was going to happen next.

No one seemed to notice. They were too busy with Mrs. Fargo to worry about a kid.

"I've tried everything," Dr. Drucker told the secretary as he hung up the phone. "I hate to do it to them, but I have no choice. The superintendent is sending Mr. Marrs in to take care of those troublesome sixth graders."

"Mr. Marrs? Oh, my!" The secretary put her hand to her face in disbelief.

A hush fell over the office. Finally, Dr. Drucker repeated, "Marrs."

Slowly, quietly, I slid off the couch. Carefully I opened and closed the office door. I raced down the hall as fast as I could.

Left without a teacher, our class was going crazy. Paper airplanes sailed through the air. A spitball hit me in the face.

"What happened in the office?" Nicho yelled.

"Fargo's not coming back, is she?"

I headed toward my desk. Nicho was still staring at me when I sat down. He expected an answer.

"She freaked out," I told Nicho. "Now Dr. Drucker's calling in some guy from Mars."

You could hear a pin drop.

"Mars?"

I opened up a book and pretended to read. Everyone was staring at me.

"That's what Drucker said." I gulped. Then I said it again in case they hadn't heard me the first time.

"We're going to have a substitute teacher from Mars."

CHAPTER 2

y best friend used to be Waylon Warfield. Practically every day during the summer, we leaned off the bridge near his house and caught crabs using bacon and twine. When those crabs sank their pincers into the bacon, they wouldn't let go.

Mom says I'm like a crab, because when I grab onto an idea, I won't let go either. Dad was like that, too, she says. Stubborn.

Waylon and I were great pen pals for a while after I moved to Bigelow Springs. Then Waylon kind of drifted away. I even sent him some of my drawings, but he didn't write back. Finally, I just stopped writing to him.

Now my best friend is my little brother, Tony.

Tony might be only seven years old, but he thinks I'm neat. The way he mimics me, you would think I was some big hero or something.

On Saturday, Tony and I were standing beside the lobster tank in the supermarket in Bigelow Springs. Crawling at the bottom of the tank and peering out at us with their beady little eyes were three big, juicy lobsters.

"Want me to show you how Waylon and I went crabbing?" I asked Tony.

Tony's blue eyes grew round as saucers. "Yeah!"

Being careful that no one was watching, I pulled a piece of twine out of my pocket. Attached to the twine was the rubber worm Nicho had used the day before on a substitute teacher.

"This might not work," I told Tony just in case. Normally, I like everything to be perfect. But since Mom didn't keep bacon in the refrigerator anymore, I would have to improvise.

The next thing I knew, a man's hand clamped down hard on my shoulder. A deep voice announced Mom's name over the loudspeaker.

"Will Marcia Donatelli please report to the Seafood Department."

Tony bounced up and down. He waved his arms and yelled, "Hey, that's Mom's name! Somebody wants Mom!"

Sometimes I think it might be better if I had a best friend closer to my own age.

Judging by his stern look, the lobster man expected Mom to be mad as hornets. But she wasn't.

"A plastic worm!" Mom held onto her sides and laughed until tears ran down her cheeks. "Oh, honey, why didn't you tell me you were hungry for lobster?

Maybe we'll buy lobster for his birthday," she told the lobster man.

Afterward Mom let Tony push the cart. The way Tony acted, you'd have thought having Mom's name announced on the loudspeaker made us famous. He kept dancing up to people. If they didn't already know who Mom was, he told them.

"Can't you make him stop?" I was afraid some of the kids from school might be watching.

"Why? Look at all the fun he's having." Mom tossed a bag of pretzels in the cart. "Honestly, Jerry. You absolutely amaze me with your ideas."

Later when I helped Mom unpack the groceries, she made a big deal out of inspecting the bags for plastic worms.

She turned a bag upside down and shook it before letting it drop to the floor. "Nope, no creepy-crawlies here! Maybe I should search your pockets."

Mom is as quick as lightning. Before I knew it, she had me in a bear hug and was tickling me.

"Quit it, Mom. No fair. You're bigger than me."

"Not much!"

"You're fatter than me!" I knew that would get her.

"Hey! I am not!"

"You might as well be!" I was laughing. "Either way, I can't fight back."

Meanwhile, Tony was at the sink introducing Rusty to fresh lettuce. Rusty is Tony's turtle.

"Hey, Mom," I croaked. "Rusty's eating all our lettuce!"

When Mom loosened her grasp, I quickly wriggled free.

Mom laid six pieces of bread on a cutting board. She opened up a jar of peanut butter. "Okay, so did you decide where we're going after lunch?"

Every Saturday after helping Mom with the groceries, Tony and I take turns picking a fun place we want to go. Sometimes it's a movie at the town center or video games at the mall. This week it was my turn to choose.

"The library," I said.

Tony set his milk on the counter. "But we went to the library last time."

"So? I want to go there again."

I was still shaken up about that guy from Mars the superintendent was sending over to handle our classroom. I needed as much information as possible on the planet Mars.

That evening, I was reading a library book at the kitchen table while Tony slurped up his spaghetti one strand at a time. Every once in a while, Tony would do something funny like slurp a noodle halfway. Then he would open his mouth and, grabbing his neck like he was choking, let the single strand hang out.

I have taught Tony some pretty neat tricks.

"Do you know anything about a teacher from Mars?" I asked Mom when she popped into the kitchen to see how we were doing. She was getting ready for her date.

"Interesting name. I think we might have had a science teacher by the name of Marrs. If it's the one I'm thinking of, he blew up the laboratory and disappeared.

But probably it's not the same man. As I recall, Mr. Marrs was very short. Only an inch or so taller than me."

I was still reading about Mars when Mom's date came to pick her up. Since my dad died, my mom has only gone out on dates maybe a half dozen times. The guys have all been creepazoids.

This one wasn't much better.

Tony stood on the couch and peered up at him. "Are you the Headless Horseman?" Tony asked. If Mom had heard, she would have made Tony apologize.

"Ho, ho, ho," was the Headless Horseman's answer. Then he ruffled my hair.

It bugs me the way Mom's dates ruffle my hair like I'm a little kid. Tony doesn't mind when they do it to him, but it drives me nuts.

"Now, remember, Jerry," Mom said. "You're in charge of entertaining Tony. Be sure you get to bed on time. We'll be at the movies. Here's the number if you need me."

Whenever Mom goes out, it's my job to amuse Tony with neat games and projects. At bedtime I usually read him a story. Tonight, I thought I'd try something different.

"How about if I make up a story about Martians with laser guns and green slime that peels off their faces?" I suggested.

"Cool, Jerry!" Tony bolted up the steps. He started jumping on the mattress and shouting, "Martians! Martians! Martians!"

I waited until the bouncing stopped before I sat down on the edge of the bed. To go along with the story, I drew pictures of Martians that had beady little eyes and strange pincers for arms.

The more I spun my story, the closer Tony sat. He grabbed his blanket and stuck his thumb in his mouth.

"Hey, don't worry," I said. "It's just a story. There's no such thing as Martians. We both know that."

There wasn't any point in scaring Tony even more by telling him that Dr. Drucker was sending somebody from Mars to teach our class.

I waited until Tony was asleep before I turned on the television. Talk about luck. There was a program on about UFO sightings, using home videos people had taken of flying saucers.

I put my feet up on the couch and leaned back. The next thing I knew a Martian smelling strangely of microwave popcorn loomed over me.

I tried to scream. Before I could move, the Martian reached back with his clawed hand and peeled a layer of green slime off his face. Gross! His face oozed with melted lava.

"Take me to your leader," he demanded and shoved a laser gun in my side.

He could only mean Nicho. Nicho was the leader of our class at school.

I woke up in a cold sweat, my T-shirt sticking to my back.

Whew! It was a good thing I didn't *really* believe in Martians.

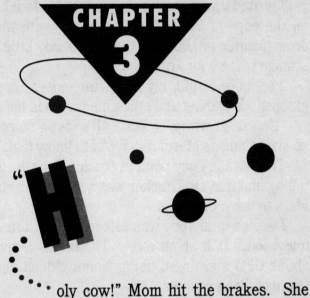

CHAPTER 3

"H oly cow!" Mom hit the brakes. She was driving Tony and me to school like she does every morning.

R-rrrrooom. R-rrrroooom.

Tony's head was hanging out of the back window. "Cool! It's a motorcycle," Tony shouted, as if we would have guessed otherwise.

A Harley swerved past our car and sputtered into the teachers' parking lot. I glanced back, expecting a big guy with a beard and at least one earring.

Quickly, I drew my hand up to use as a visor as bolts of lightning shot through the air. Then I saw it was only the sun's rays reflecting off the biker's silver helmet.

"Why is that man at our school?" Tony asked. "Is he somebody's daddy?"

"Don't be a goofball," I answered for Mom. "When's the last time you saw a dad ride up on a motorcycle?"

"Christopher's daddy came on a fire truck."

"Christoper's daddy worked for the fire department." Mom winked at me. She appreciated that.

While Tony and I watched, the biker unstrapped a black sports bag from behind his seat. Now he was strolling through the parking lot, heading for the front of the building.

Talk about weird. In his shiny green jacket, green pants, and white moon boots, he looked like somebody . . .

From Mars!

I couldn't help myself. I giggled out loud. If that was our new substitute, Nicho was in over his head!

Nicho was probably thinking the same thing.

As the substitute from Mars entered the front door, I spotted Nicho leaning against the building, one leg propped behind him, both arms folded across his chest.

He was, as usual, looking cool. I could only imagine what he must be thinking.

If our class didn't make the *Guinness Book of World Records*, Nicho's name would be M.U.D.

"See you tonight, kiddos. Give me a kiss," Mom said as I popped open the car door.

Tony leaned across the backseat to give Mom a hug and a kiss. She only winked at me, which is a signal we have since big kids don't always like to kiss their moms in public.

As usual there was no teacher on guard in our

classroom. Substitutes have to report to Dr. Drucker on their first day. Our substitutes only last one day.

"Hey, wait till you get a load of this new dude," Nicho said as he swaggered to his desk. Right away Kelly perked up. I noticed because she was standing next to Sharon.

Sharon has long black hair. And she's pretty, really pretty, especially when she smiles.

Sharon and Kelly are best friends.

With a loud smack, Nicho's knapsack landed on his desk. "I'm telling you. This weirdo is from outer space."

"Greetings!"

A man not much taller than my mother stood framed in the doorway. A black sports bag was slung over his shoulder. He had a silver helmet tucked under his arm, and he was was carrying a pair of white moon boots.

My heart beat a mile a minute as the man's head slowly rotated on his neck, taking us all in.

Behind me, someone gasped.

Satisfied, our new sub walked briskly to the teacher's desk. He dropped his helmet, boots, and bag in the corner. Then, popping his suspenders, he picked up a piece of chalk.

"Chalk!" He held it high over his head like we might never have seen a piece of chalk before. "Soft white, gray, or buff limestone chiefly composed of the shells of foraminifers."

"What the . . ." Nicho mumbled under his breath.

"Let's get out of here while we still can," Victor muttered back.

I tried slinking further down in my seat.

"Whoooops!" The piece of chalk rolled across the floor. But before I could blink, the chalk magically reappeared in the teacher's hand.

For the first time since Mrs. Meriweather left on maternity leave, our class was dead quiet.

"Aha! Introductions." The sub's voice boomed against the silence.

While we watched transfixed, he pressed his fingers to his forehead like he was tuning in to some other frequency. Then, turning his back to the class he wrote

MR. MARRS

in big letters on the chalkboard.

Beside me, Nicho coughed nervously. He rested his elbow on his desk and whispered, "I smeared honey on his chair. Don't worry. We'll get rid of this weirdo real quick."

"Maybe. Maybe not," Freddie said.

Nicho was confident. "Wait till Marrs sits down."

The whole morning, we waited for Mr. Marrs to sit down. Instead, he flitted around the room looking for a place to land. He tiptoed between our desks. He leaned against the bookshelves. He half sat on the air conditioning unit. He stared out the windows. He inspected our science projects. Later, he stepped into the hallway to get a drink of water. But he never once sat in his chair.

He never even *looked* at his chair. It was like his chair never existed.

By eleven o'clock, Nicho was going buggy. He was jerking his shoulders and shuffling his feet on the floor, locking his shoes around the chair in front of him.

I gave him a sideways glare when he started nervously clicking his pen.

"Book drop eleven-fifteen," Nicho whispered. "Pass it on."

It went around the room like wildfire.

I started watching the clock when the first book dropped at eleven-eleven. Somebody got anxious.

"Hey, I said eleven-fifteen, stupid!"

Four minutes later Nicho's elbow edged across his desk. Bang! His math book hit the floor.

Bang! Bang! Freddie's and Victor's were the next to go, followed by seventeen others. Bang! Bang! Bang!

Mr. Marrs never looked up.

Nicho scowled. The pen clicking accelerated.

"Cover for me," he whispered to Freddie.

Right away, Freddie's hand shot up. Mr. Marrs was at Freddie's desk in a flash. Then, while Freddie asked Mr. Marrs stupid questions about this week's spelling words, Nicho dropped a fake tarantula on the teacher's desk.

There is not a substitute teacher in this world that likes a tarantula.

It seemed like a good time to go to the bathroom.

On my way back to my chair, I peeked at the

teacher's desk. A hairy spider foot was stepping out from under the seating chart. As soon as he went to his desk, Marrs would spot the tarantula. As usual, Nicho had done a super job.

I sat down and waited.

Forty-five minutes later, we returned from P. E. Obviously, Mr. Marrs had not sat down nor noticed the tarantula.

Instead, he was standing at the door and beckoning us in. He was smiling, clapping his hands, and calling each of us by name. "How glad I am to see you, Jerry. I've missed you, Nicho. Welcome, Kelly. Sharon, what took you so long?"

Something was drastically wrong. Where was this substitute coming from? Nobody ever missed Nicho!

Before I knew it, it was time for lunch.

Sharon was sitting between Kelly and Victor in the cafeteria when Nicho leaned over Kelly's shoulder and took a French fry off her tray.

"Stop that, you goon."

"Baboon!"

Most of the time, you could tell Kelly really liked Nicho. Like now, she was batting her eyelashes and swatting him on the shoulder.

Nicho only laughed. He pulled a chair out and plopped down. Victor leaned across the table. "Now what?"

"Don't sweat it. Dr. Drucker must have given the guy the message. He knew enough not to sit down and he knew the tarantula was a fake. Dead Bug will get him."

"Two o'clock, right?" Victor asked.

"No! Wrong."

The kids were stunned. "Wrong?"

"Right," Nicho said. "Wrong."

Victor scratched his head. "Hey, what do you mean, right, wrong? You just said . . . "

"I said not at two o'clock. Wise up, would you? If Marrs knew about the chair and he knew about the spider, what's to say he doesn't know about Dead Bug?"

Nicho blew bubbles in his milk. "Instead of two o'clock, we'll do Dead Bug at two-thirty."

"Smart." Victor spit an orange seed across the table. "Yeah. Just when the sub's thinking he's made it through the day with us, bang-o!"

No way was I going to the nurse's office for my allergy medicine today. I didn't want to miss anything.

At two o'clock, Dr. Drucker dropped by to see how our new sub was surviving sixth grade. Looking smug, Nicho nodded his head, rubbed his chin, and leaned way back in his chair. He was in his glory.

At exactly two-thirty, Nicho, Victor, and Freddie keeled over. Kelly was next to drop, followed by Sharon, me, and everybody else.

We rolled over on our backs and started kicking the air with our feet and waving our arms like a bunch of exterminated cockroaches.

Out of the corner of my eye I saw Sharon giggling, kicking, and having a great time. Meanwhile, Marrs kept reading aloud from our weekly current events newspaper.

"Kick harder. Wiggle!" Nicho whispered hoarsely.

I tried kicking harder. I even tried to wiggle. But the floors they build for sixth graders are hard. Besides, I don't exactly have the muscles to kick and wave like a dead bug for much longer than three minutes. I doubt real dead bugs kick and wave that long.

Apparently, I wasn't the only bug with a problem. After five minutes of frantic kicking, waving, and wiggling a couple of the girls started to whine.

"My back hurts."

"This isn't any fun. Can't we get up?"

"Yeah, Nicho. We don't want to do this anymore."

Fortunately for Nicho, the first bell rang for dismissal. But we were still on the floor. And Marrs was still reading!

Nicho's face was red as a tomato. "Okay. Everybody back in their seats."

When the second bell rang, Marrs finally put the newspaper down. He snapped his suspenders. "That's a wrap, folks! Enjoy your evening. Oh yes . . ." By now everyone was gawking at the peculiar little man in the popping red suspenders. "Thanks for a great day!"

Thanks for a great day?

Nicho was the first to dash out the door. It wasn't as easy for me. My legs were stiff. Sort of like an out-of-practice dead bug.

Somehow I managed to gather my things and limp away from the dark and mysterious world of dead bugs and Mr. Marrs and into the bright afternoon sun.

Even though Mom drives us to school, Tony and I always walk home. It's not far and Mom says the exercise does us good. She usually rolls into our driveway a few minutes after we get there. If she beats us home, I'm in real trouble. No excuses. I'm in charge of making sure that Tony doesn't dawdle.

Tony and I always meet on the playground right across from the teachers' parking lot. Usually, only little kids use the playground after school, but today Nicho was there with a bunch of other guys.

Seeing me, Tony yanked at my jacket. "What's going on?" For a second grader, Tony doesn't miss much. He probably gets it from hanging around me.

"Nothing. Big kid stuff." Even though I knew we should start for home, I couldn't stop watching Nicho and the guys ogle Mr. Marrs's motorcycle.

It didn't take long before Mr. Marrs trotted past in his green outfit with the white moon boots. While we stood there, popping gum and doing our best to look busy, Marrs buckled his silver helmet on his head, threw his leg over the motorcycle, and zoomed off.

R-rrrrooom. R-rrrroooom.

Suddenly, Marrs circled back into the lot. He made one of those sharp turns like you see the stunt drivers do on TV. When he stopped he was staring straight at us.

Long seconds passed. He revved his Harley.

R-rrrrooom. R-rrrroooom.

Then, right in the middle of the teachers' parking lot, with half a million lightning bolts shooting out of his head, Marrs sat up straight and tall in his shiny green uniform. Before anyone could say a word, Marrs brought his hand stiffly to his green chest. Then, keeping his arm level, he gave us a snappy space salute.

Holy smokes!

Before I could blink, he was gone.

"You might as well say good-bye to Dork Brain because we won't see him again," Nicho said in a loud voice.

That wasn't something I would have put money on.

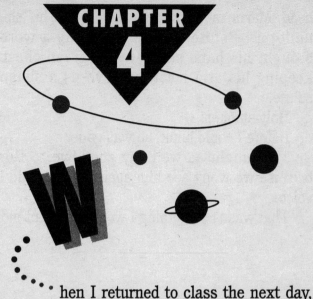

CHAPTER 4

hen I returned to class the next day, Mr. Marrs was waiting. Obviously, someone forgot to tell him he wasn't supposed to come back.

As I headed for my desk, he was sitting in the chair Nicho had smeared with honey. He was bent over and writing something in a tablet.

"Washed it off slick as a whistle."

I almost dropped my teeth. Had Marrs read my mind?

"You betcha."

I plopped in my seat, unwilling to believe what had happened. According to the schedule on the board, we were supposed to be following Marrs's example and writing in our journals. I started by drawing a picture of Mr. Marrs reading my mind.

I glanced in Sharon's direction. Kelly was tapping

her forehead with her pencil. She raised her hand.

"No, Kelly," Marrs said. "Journals are very private. I won't be reading yours and you won't be reading mine."

Kelly sucked in her breath. Her face turned pale.

A faint smile twitched across the substitute's face. "Go ahead, folks. Continue recording your thoughts and observations while I do the same."

I changed the drawing so Mr. Marrs was reading a whole class full of minds besides my own.

"Okay, folks. We have a lot to cover today," Marrs said, dropping his journal in the top drawer of his desk. He began pacing around the room and snapping his suspenders.

Meanwhile Freddie egged Nicho on. "Go ahead. I dare you. Tell Marrs we get a two-hour break."

"Nah. He'll never buy it."

Mr. Marrs pressed his fingers to his forehead. "Mars to Earth. Mars to Earth. Come in, earthlings."

Right away Freddie straightened. Nicho's face turned bright red and my stomach flip-flopped about a million times.

Marrs dropped his arms and smiled.

"Take out your math books and turn to page 163."

Across from me, Nicho hunched over and cupped his hand around his mouth. "Pssst, Robertson. Meet me in the boys' room. I'll go first."

Wilber Robertson leaned back in his chair and nodded as Marrs continued writing on the chalkboard.

"Yes, Nicho. You may visit the boys' room." Marrs

said it without bothering to turn around.

Startled, Nicho jumped up. He tucked his shirt into his jeans. "Yo," he mumbled. "I guess I was going there."

"Wilber, you're excused, too. You boys be quick about it. All of you folks need to complete this math test before lunch or you'll get a zero."

A few minutes later, Nicho returned to the classroom. But instead of going to his desk, he made a beeline straight to Wilber's.

Meanwhile Wilber slid through the door and tapped Freddie on the shoulder, and Freddie moved over to Sharon's desk. The room hummed with excitement. Then Sharon's chair scraped the floor and fell over with a loud crash. Sharon stood up and shyly covered her face with her hands.

For a second, everyone held their breath, waiting to see what Marrs would do.

What was going on? He didn't do anything!

Finally, Sharon stepped backward, letting Freddie take her seat.

Everyone kept switching until no one was seated in their own desk. Except me. I was the only one who wasn't tapped.

Suddenly, Marrs stopped. He cleared his throat.

Everyone looked up, expecting him to turn on his heels and completely freak out.

Instead, he stood there with his back to the class and slowly moved his head from side to side. While we stared, completely spellbound, he ruffled a pencil through the hair on the back of his head.

Holy cow! A pair of green eyeballs darted back and forth. And then . . . the eyeballs settled on me!

"From what I can see, Jerry, you alone remain the center of our universe—the only stationary body in this whole entire galaxy. Observe! Wouldn't you say our other planets are careening wildly out of control?"

It was a teacher's question, the kind kids weren't supposed to answer. Besides, there wasn't time.

The substitute's eyes (the green ones in back of his head) had darted to Nicho.

"Nicho. You left your orbit a long time ago."

Kelly's hand covered her mouth in shock. At the same time, Nicho croaked. He slumped in his chair like a dead man.

My stomach was churning so badly I thought I might be sick.

After lunch, Marrs was back again.

"Okay, folks. You know me, I'm full of surprises!"

I didn't think Marrs needed to remind us.

"Now we're going to cover our weather assignment using imagination!" Marrs emphasized with a flourish. He wrote the word on the chalkboard.

IMAGINATION

Mr. Marrs stepped to the window and opened it. Gazing outside, he began rubbing his temples and muttering in a language nobody else could understand.

"Zzzz xxx ooop dee dooo zzzs tsfffprt sshe rrxxxt."

"What the . . . "

Freddie edged closer to the window. "There's no one out there. Who's he talking to?"

Nicho clicked his pen nervously. "What's he using, radio waves?"

But there was no radio we could see, unless Marrs had one implanted inside his head.

"Hey, look at the computer!" Victor shouted. "No one touched it, but it's blinking. It wasn't even on a minute ago."

Marrs whirled on his heels. His hand pointed at the computer, and the printer started printing.

"What the . . ." Nicho was the first to reach the printer. "Huh? It's a weather report."

Marrs popped his suspenders. "You know me, full of surprises," he said again. "How many of you want to put together a skit?"

Hands shot up right away.

"We'll break into groups. I'll call out different kinds of weather. You choose what you want to be. Then go to different sections of the room to plan your skits."

Marrs began calling out, "Rain. Blizzard. Tornado. Hurricane, Drought. Dust storms." He paused. "Be careful. If there's anything I know quite a bit about, it's dust storms."

The way he said that set off little warning signals in my head. But there wasn't time to worry about that now.

A couple of minutes later I went to the front of the room with the rest of the tornadoes, including Sharon.

While we quickly prepared our skits, Marrs snapped

his suspenders and shouted encouragement as he moved from group to group. "We don't know what's going to happen next. This is going to be super. Absolutely super!"

A cyclone of activity had hit our classroom. Everything and everyone was moving at once. While Marrs was busy, we opened up the supply cabinet. Someone grabbed a pack of magic markers and shoved a purple one at me.

"Use this. It's washable."

Quickly, I streaked purple marker all over my face and up and down my arms. I bunched my hair together with rubber bands, then checked myself in the mirror. Terrific! Three clumps of hair stood straight up like they'd been caught in a funnel cloud.

Sharon looked at me and blinked like she couldn't believe what she saw. "Your mother is going to kill you."

She meant the purple marker. "It's washable," I told her.

The hurricanes were first. Nicho was supposed to be a house. Kelly, Paul, and Leigh whirled around and shook like a bunch of trees. Then they picked Nicho up and carried him across the room.

When it was our turn everyone made wind noises. I waited until the wind got really loud. Then I burst into the center of the room, leaped into the air, and landed light as a feather on my toes.

I'd seen a tornado once when I was crabbing with Waylon. I remembered how the sky had looked green and the air had filled with a peculiar sulphur smell. All around, the world stood still, just like later when my father died. Then, suddenly, the leaves stood on end and there was a huge roar. I remembered Waylon's scream as we ran and crouched under the bridge. We weren't even in the tornado's path. But we might as well have been, it was that scary.

Now, as the other kids began making wind noises, I could feel myself becoming that tornado.

From somewhere far away, I heard girls shriek as I leaped into the air. When I came down, I did a few karate kicks and chops. Quickly, I spun away. Next I leaped onto a desk and back to the floor again.

I don't know what got into me.

I did a tornado whirl and landed right in front of Sharon. Sharon blushed and backed up. I went after her, whirling and twirling, and throwing out karate kicks.

Then, just so she wouldn't be too scared, I shook my hips and did the hoochie coochie.

When it was over, kids were screaming and clapping. Sharon was smiling.

"I'm proud of all of the groups. Let's assign some grades," Mr. Marrs said when we'd finished our skits.

Hurricanes, Dust Storms, and Blizzards got an A minus. Tornadoes got an A plus.

"Okay, folks! We need to move on!" Marrs said, slapping the grade book shut. "Everyone in this school is decorating their door for the Spirit Week contest, and we want to win with the best door, right? We want to be Number One in the universe!"

"Let's go for it!" someone shouted.

Girls madly waved their arms. Everyone had an idea. Except me.

I was busy drawing a picture of the planet Mars in my spiral binder. I had a bunch of red asteroids flying around and, in the background, I had the moons, Phobos and Deimos. In the foreground, I sketched a crashed spaceship and a vehicle with a United States flag. In the corner was a flying saucer with tiny square windows. A couple of little green Martians stood around holding laser guns.

I felt Mr. Marrs's eyes on me—the blue pair on the front of his face. I hadn't even heard him step up to my desk, but there he was, peering over my shoulder and inspecting my drawing.

Quickly, I slid my left hand over my paper. I started to turn the page but Marrs wouldn't let me.

Slowly he moved his finger across the picture until it stopped at the flying saucer.

"Hmmmm," he said. "May I?"

I wasn't about to say no.

"Sure," I gulped.

Using the side of his finger he quickly erased the tiny square windows. Just as fast—but using his fingernail now—he drew in a dome light with lines to show it was blinking.

"Oh." I coughed nervously.

He glided past my desk. Then, looking over his shoulder, he smiled and winked knowingly. He put his index finger and thumb together to make the A-OK sign.

"What the . . . did you see that?" For the second time that afternoon, Nicho's mouth dropped almost to the floor.

Sharon and Kelly were both in shock.

I couldn't stop staring at my drawing. How did Marrs do that? He hadn't used an eraser. He hadn't used a pencil. He'd used his finger.

"Okay, folks!" When Marrs snapped his suspenders, we all jumped. "We may have the theme for our door back there on our young artist's desk. What do you think, folks? Shall we use the planet Mars? You'd be surprised how much I know about Mars."

Across from me, Nicho sucked in his breath.

CHAPTER 5

o one could believe it. We'd never had a substitute teacher return for a second week. No one in our class was saying it out loud, but no normal human being would put up with the abuse Nicho and the other kids in our class dished out. There was only one possible explanation. Marrs had to be an alien in human form.

But why was he here in Bigelow Springs? What did he want with us?

By now we'd given up on Dead Bug, dropping books, and switching seats. We'd tapped our pencils, clicked our pens, and batted spitballs every time Marrs turned his back, but we got no reaction from him.

Besides the tarantula, Nicho tried laying a rubber snake on Marrs's desk. Victor brought in a fake apple. Freddie's dribble glass only made Marrs laugh. One of the girls set a whoopie cushion on the teacher's chair and somebody else tried plastic throw-up.

Every day in the cafeteria, Nicho predicted that Marrs was just a step away from disappearing off the face of the Earth.

Most of us weren't so sure.

The strain took its toll on Nicho. His left eye twitched and his hair stuck out like a porcupine's quills.

"If this substitute *is* from Mars . . ." Nicho paused. His eye twitched as he nervously ran his fingers through his hair.

Everyone was getting testy, including Sharon. She flung her black hair behind her shoulder. "This is really dumb. There's no such thing as aliens."

"Then how come he doesn't know the Pledge of Allegiance?" Nicho demanded. "I've watched him, and he only says the last couple of words: 'With liberty and justice for all.' "

Kelly jumped in. "So what? I don't say half the words either."

"What about the extra pair of eyes he has in the back of his head?" Nicho yelled.

"Honestly, Nicho! You never saw eyes on the back of his head." Kelly's hands were on her hips.

"Okay, okay. So I imagined it," Nicho said, backing down. "But what about the day when he erased Donatelli's drawing with his finger, then drew a new one with that same finger? It was like he had an eraser and pencil built in. Explain that!"

For the first time Sharon sounded uncertain. "Mr. Marrs did seem to know what spaceships look like, and he did help Jerry make his drawings for Spirit Week look awfully real."

"Which is exactly why Mars is keeping Donatelli's drawings. They remind him of home. I say the guy is from Mars."

Kelly rolled her eyes. "Okay, Nicho. I tell you what. Maybe you could get us in the *Guinness Book of World Records* for being the only sixth-grade class with a substitute teacher from Mars." She stood up and pushed her chair under the table. "C'mon, Sharon," she said.

"Wait a second." Nicho grabbed Kelly's arm. "I can prove it. We'll try taking a picture of Marrs. Everyone knows you can't take a Martian's picture."

Kelly giggled. "You're thinking of vampires. You're more confused than we thought."

Nicho pretended not to hear. "So, Sharon," he said, "you have a camera. Bring it in tomorrow."

"I can't. It's my dad's and he won't let me borrow it."

"What about you?" Nicho looked at Freddie.

Freddie shook his head, no.

"You?"

Not Billy either.

I don't know what made me say it. "My mom has a Polaroid."

"Yo, Donatelli!" Nicho boomed. "I like your attitude!" He clapped me on the back so hard I almost passed out.

The rest of the afternoon Nicho told everyone how my mom's Polaroid was the perfect choice. We wouldn't have to wait around to get the film developed. We'd have a picture of the alien in our hot little hands tomorrow afternoon.

I waited until Mom and Tony were cleaning up the supper dishes to sneak into Mom's closet. Quietly, I pulled a chair away from her desk. If I stood on the chair and stretched, I could reach the camera.

Stuffing the Polaroid under my shirt, I scooted back upstairs and slid it into my backpack.

If Mom knew I'd borrowed something from her without asking first, I'd be grounded for the rest of my life.

But it was worth the risk.

The next morning, Nicho was leaning against the brick wall outside of school. "Yo, Donatelli. You got the camera?"

I tapped my backpack. "In here."

"You checked it out to make sure it works, right?"

I hated to admit that I hadn't.

"No sweat." Nicho threw his arm over my shoulder as Sharon and Kelly appeared out of nowhere.

I waited until Sharon smiled. Then I clicked the shutter. If my ears had gotten any hotter, they would have melted.

"My uncle has a camera like this one," Kelly said. "You have to pull this little white tab and be careful not to touch the picture." She frowned. "Hey, I thought you were taking a picture of both of us."

"The camera must have moved." It was the best excuse I could think of.

As soon as we got upstairs Nicho hollered, "Yo, Mr.

Marrs. We need a picture of you and the rest of us standing in front of our door. You know, with the ribbon showing we won first prize."

Marrs straightened up. "I don't think so. My pictures never turn out."

"Oh, come on. It's for the school yearbook."

The girls were already lined up beside the door. Meanwhile, Nicho was making a face like Marrs was only confirming what Nicho had said all along.

Overruled, Marrs stepped into the hallway.

I put the camera against my nose and peeked through the tiny square opening. "Move closer so I can get you all in." I indicated with my hand where everyone should go.

"I'm telling you, I take lousy pictures," Marrs repeated.

I clicked the shutter. I was trembling so badly I thought I might tear the white tab, but I didn't.

Slowly, the exposure became clearer and clearer.

Nicho had two fingers over Freddie's head. Sharon was smiling sweetly and Kelly's eyes were closed. Right where Mr. Marrs was supposed to be standing was a bright green streak.

"Hey, what happened?" I asked. "Everyone else in the picture is just fine."

"Sorry, guys." Marrs didn't seem a bit surprised. "I told you, for some peculiar reason my pictures never come out."

Puzzled, I turned the camera over, inspecting it. No doubt about it. Something awfully strange was going on.

CHAPTER 6

"say this time we do something crazy. Really crazy," Nicho said. "So crazy it fires him up and he has to go!"

We were in the library. Bringing Mom's camera to school had automatically made me a part of Nicho's crowd.

"Like what?" I asked.

"Yeah, what's left?" Billy chimed in.

Kelly sounded frustrated. "We've done almost everything we know how to do."

Nicho snapped his notebook shut. He raised his eyebrows and smiled. "After lunch, we turn all our clothes inside out."

"I don't want to do that," Kelly shrieked.

"Shhhhh!" Sharon whispered.

"I don't care. My folks spend lots of money on my

clothes. I don't want to look like a bum."

"Okay, then we do this." Nicho slid cards of thumbtacks around the table. "Go ahead. Take some tacks and put them in your shoes. My brother did it to a dopey sub he had in high school."

Victor reached over Freddie's shoulder and grabbed a card. He ripped the cellophane off. "Won't it hurt?"

"The outside of your shoes, dum-dum. When we walk around the classroom, the tacks will make clicking noises. It's going to drive Marrs nuts."

Freddie put six tacks in each of his shoes.

I put the same amount in mine.

"Ohh, this is better than the clothes thing. This is going to be so cool." Kelly put a handful in hers.

Nicho used almost a whole card of tacks.

When we left the library, we were giggling, slapping each other on the back, and sounding like tap dancers.

"Okay, folks, up and at 'em!" Marrs clapped his hands. "Everyone standing! That's it! Time to fuel those thought waves!"

"What the . . . "

Marrs snapped his suspenders. He did the moon-walk. Suddenly he stopped and shouted.

"And jump out!" His arms and legs went out.

"Jump in!" His arms and legs went in.

We were supposed to do the same. Legs out. Legs in. With tacks in our shoes, we were skidding all over the place. Kelly crashed into her desk and almost fell down.

"Arms up! Arms down!" Marrs went on for *five* minutes.

Finally, Marrs shouted, "Collapse!"

I peered over at Nicho. We were both huffing and puffing like dead bugs.

"If you ask me, this whole thing is crazy," Sharon said later at lunch.

"What?" Nicho asked, pretending not to know what Sharon was getting at.

"Thumbtacks, Dead Bug, and all the other stupid stunts. It's so immature."

"Yeah, well, who would have figured on getting someone like Mr. Marrs for a sub. The man's not human. He's ... he's a Martian," Nicho blurted.

Everyone groaned.

That's the difference between Nicho and me. If I said anything about Martians, the kids would have laughed. With Nicho, the most they did was groan.

Even so, Nicho was riled. His troops were rebelling.

"I'm not kidding. I already proved it with Donatelli's camera. What more do you want?" Nicho argued. "When we go back inside, you watch him, because I'm telling you, the man is an alien in human form."

Kelly began making strange beeping noises. "Beep-beep-beep-beep ..."

"I say we gather clues to confirm our suspicions," Nicho kept on.

"And if he is?" somebody asked.

"Then we tell someone. Maybe the chief of police or the president of the United States."

Victor made a telephone out of his hand and put it to his ear. "Hello, Mr. President. I know you're interested in different cultures, but did you know we have a Martian for a substitute teacher?"

I crunched my milk carton, shoved it in my lunchbag, and glared at Nicho. "Nobody is going to believe us because our class has caused too much trouble. We've got a bad rep."

Nicho pursed his lips. He let out a determined breath. "That's exactly why we have to document what we've seen in one long, detailed, organized list. If anyone sees anything suspicious, tell . . ." Nicho glanced around the table before settling on me.

"Donatelli!" he whooped. "He'll put everything together. Then when we're ready, we'll take our proof to Dr. Drucker."

Everyone shouted at once.

"Hey, Donatelli! Write what Marrs said on Monday about having a case of jet lag from zooming all over the place."

I whipped a pen out of my shirt pocket. Since I didn't have any paper with me, I made little notes on my hand.

Freddie's nose was in my face. "Get this. I heard Marrs tell a teacher how he needed a suitable habitat with a spacious garage—vital for his experiments."

Sharon's voice was quieter. "His watch keeps stopping."

Kelly leaned across the table. "And when I asked him how old he was he said he didn't count age in years the way earthlings do. We're supposed to think of him as a day older than yesterday and a day younger than tomorrow."

I had already written on the back of my hand and the palm. I rolled up my shirt sleeve and was working my way up my arm when the bell rang.

Back in the classroom, Marrs had his index fingers pressed to his forehead again. "Mars to Earth. Mars to Earth. Come in, earthlings."

Twitching out of control, Nicho made a writing motion with his hand. "Do it, Donatelli."

I pulled my binder out of my desk and flipped to a clean sheet of paper. Glancing at the notes on my hand and arm, I frantically began to write.

icho had given me a lousy job. I barely had time to eat my lunch, go to the bathroom, or enjoy recess. Kids constantly bugged me with suspicious facts.

Of course, I had already uncovered a few suspicious facts of my own.

The first occurred when Mr. Marrs abruptly stopped in his tracks as he led us toward the lunchroom.

"What on earth is that smell?" He was rubbing his stomach and sniffing the air.

I looked at Nicho. Nicho looked at me. We both stared at Mr. Marrs.

"You mean pizza?" we said practically at the same time.

Marrs's eyes were puzzled. "Pizza? Hmmm. Where I come from we don't have pizza."

"Name me one place that doesn't have pizza, besides

Mars," Nicho demanded later in the cafeteria.

No one could answer that. Not even me.

I uncovered another suspicious fact during health class.

Mr. Marrs was reminding us how we should buckle our seatbelts when Sharon raised her hand. "What about motorcycle helmets?"

Marrs agreed. "My stars! If you drive a motorcycle, you must always wear a helmet. That goes for riding bikes, too."

Sharon wrinkled her nose. "Doesn't your head get hot?"

Mr. Marrs leaned back against his desk. He crossed his feet at the ankles.

"You know me," he said. "I'm most comfortable wearing my helmet. In fact, my helmet makes me feel right at home."

Across from me, Nicho made beeping noises into his fist.

But the most suspicious fact of all was how Mr. Marrs kept our class on Mrs. Meriweather's schedule. No one else had been able to do that. Only a substitute from Mars could have that power.

In social studies, Mr. Marrs had us studying maps of the United States.

"Folks, we're going to begin a group project," Marrs said. "I'm going to assign each of you to a group of four. Each group will have a state to study and make a model of out of papier-mâché. You can do some of the work in class, but most of it will have to be done outside of school. If you start today, you should have plenty of time to do your research and make arrangements to work at each other's houses. You'll have two weeks to complete your project."

We've had group projects before. Most of the kids like it when we work in groups, probably because it's a good excuse to goof off.

"Jerry, I've assigned you to work with Nicho, Sharon, and Kelly. Your state is Florida."

I started to raise my hand. I had to tell Mr. Marrs he'd made a mistake. Mrs. Meriweather always let me work independently. I didn't like working with other people, at least not where grades were concerned. Mrs. Meriweather said it was because I liked to do my own thing.

I let her think that.

The real reason was that I had only gotten three B's in my whole life. The rest of my marks were always A's. I didn't want to chance getting another B — or lower.

Sharon got pretty good grades and Kelly's were okay. But Nicho's were horrible. Working on a project with him guaranteed I'd fail sixth grade.

I waited until the bell rang for dismissal. As soon as the kids left the room, I walked slowly up to Mr. Marrs's desk. Instead of using a pencil, he was grading papers with his finger.

It was hard not to stare.

Finally, I cleared my throat. "Um, Mr. Marrs."

He looked up and smiled.

"Yes, Jerry."

"I think you might have made a mistake."

He glanced down at the paper he was grading.

"Not on the test, Mr. Marrs. I think you made a mistake with me."

Marrs's smile grew wider.

"Mrs. Meriweather always let me work independently."

"Yes, and you work very well independently. But this is a group project and it would be a little difficult to work independently in a group, don't you agree?"

"I'm not like the other kids. They like to goof off. I don't. Grades matter to me."

"Grades are important, Jerry. But it's also important that you learn to work with boys and girls your own age. There is nothing wrong with being a little different. It's what you do with your difference that counts."

I was doomed. I was going to be in sixth grade for the rest of my life.

"Jerry, you have a wonderful sense of humor, and your artistic talent is quite impressive. But you have to learn to get along with your classmates. People need friends outside of their family."

It took every bit of willpower to keep from rolling my eyes. "Yeah, sure," I mumbled. I just wasn't sure why friends and schoolwork had to mix.

"My family lives miles away from here," Marrs went on. "Friends, the other teachers I work with, are very important to me."

Did he say *miles* away from here?

But I couldn't worry about that now. This alien gone berserk was destroying my life.

CHAPTER 8

om was in the living room complaining about the kids in her class giving her a headache.

"You don't know what grief kids can cause a teacher," she said.

I didn't try to dispute what she was saying. Instead, I brought her a peanut butter sandwich and a bowl of soup on a tray. I told her to lie down on the couch and put her feet up. I told her I would feed her with a spoon.

That's when she sat up and burst out laughing.

"Feed me with a spoon! I'm not sick with a fever, Jerry. I'm just sick and tired of kids who don't want to learn their Shakespeare."

"Oh, is that all?" I said.

"Is that all?" Tony mimicked. Tony was being a pest.

"It's enough. I happen to take my profession very seriously."

"What if a student said you were from Mars?"

"What?"

"Mars! Mars! Mars!" Tony was zooming around the living room like a rocket ship.

"Shut up, Tony!"

Now Mom really looked at me. I probably don't tell Tony to shut up as often as I should.

"Okay, what's going on?" Mom asked.

There wasn't time to beat around the bush. I got down on my knees and begged. I had my hands clasped. I was a desperate man.

"Mom, please! Save me! It's worse than acid indigestion. It's worse than post nasal drip. It's even worse than Preparation H. Me and three other kids have to make a map of Florida—together."

Mom shook her head and blinked.

"Mr. Marrs wants me to work with three other kids who get lousier grades than me."

Mom patted the couch. "But, Jerry, you've never received a lousy grade."

"Don't you see? I could wind up spending the rest of my life in sixth grade. Do you know how boring that will be? I'm telling you, this is a real crisis."

"I don't understand," Mom said. "Why do you think you'll need to repeat sixth grade?"

Mom was supposed to be a teacher. Why didn't she get it?

"I can take my pick. I can either do all the work

and let the other kids get the credit. Or, I can get a big fat F for Florida and be stuck in sixth grade for the rest of my life. It's not fair. You have to talk to Mr. Marrs and get him to change the assignment."

Mom sighed. "Sweetie, I can't overrule your teacher."

"Why?" I shrieked. "He's just a substitute."

"Whatever he is, I won't interfere."

I ignored for the moment what she'd said about, "whatever he is" and went straight to the heart of the matter.

"Mom, this is going to be very embarrassing for you. Here you are a teacher and your son will be growing whiskers in sixth grade."

"Like Abraham Lincoln?"

"Mom!" I wailed and headed toward my room. There ought to be a law against moms letting their eyes twinkle in the middle of an argument. It's not fair.

That night, I could hardly sleep. When I wasn't dreaming about Martians, I worried that I might show up at the wrong house. Sharon and Kelly would stand behind the living room curtains. They would see me ringing the wrong doorbell. Sharon would grab her sides and fall all over herself laughing.

This would not be cool.

The next afternoon, I pulled my bike into Sharon's driveway at almost the same moment as Nicho. Kelly's bike was already parked beside the back gate.

Just in case Kelly was trying to pull something cute with her bike, I let Nicho ring the doorbell.

A grown-up version of Sharon answered the door.

"Come in, boys," Sharon's mother said. "The girls are waiting in the basement."

When Nicho and I got downstairs, it was obvious Sharon and Kelly had definite ideas on what we would do with Florida. Sharon had already drawn a map of Florida on a piece of cardboard. It looked more like a stretched-out Christmas stocking. The way Kelly was acting, you would have thought she was in charge.

"The papier-mâché is over here," she said, pointing. "Sharon's father said we would have to put newspapers on the floor, in case we spilled anything."

While Nicho poured the water in the bowl of powdered mâché, Sharon and I spread newspapers on the floor. We kept accidentally bumping into each other and pretending we hadn't. I tried to cover Nicho's feet with newspapers.

When Nicho stomped on the papers, Kelly swatted him with a wooden spoon. "Stop acting so dumb."

Nicho looked at me and shrugged. Then he stuck both hands in the bowl of mâché.

"Oooohhhh," Kelly screamed and stuck her hands in, too.

I was next and then Sharon.

Nicho took a fistful of mâché—*Splat!*—and we had the beginnings of Florida.

Next, he glanced at the map Sharon found in an old issue of *National Geographic*. "Where should we put the mountains?"

I frowned. "There are no mountains in Florida."

"Right, there's igloos!"

I cracked up. "Igloo condominiums."

Nicho formed an igloo out of mâché. He set it in Miami. "How about a village of igloos?"

I guess Sharon thought igloo condominiums weren't such a hot idea, becuase she swooped down and snatched the igloo out of Miami. "No igloos." She handed me a plastic alligator instead.

I began making hungry alligator noises. "Hey, you guys, my alligator is eating Key West."

Before I knew it, Nicho had grabbed another alligator. We were laughing so hard we almost missed hearing Sharon's mom call us for snacks.

"You boys wash up down here," Kelly said. I guessed she'd forgotten whose house we were visiting. "Sharon and I are using the upstairs powder room."

Nicho and I shrugged. Big deal.

We were munching on popcorn and drinking our sodas in the kitchen when Sharon said, "I know this sounds silly, but I've been giving it a lot of thought and I really am afraid Mr. Marrs might be a Martian."

Sharon looked so awesome right then that I almost choked on my popcorn. Her eyelashes were as dark and shiny as her hair. My ears were burning like crazy.

"Don't worry," Kelly said, turning to Sharon. "Remember how we studied the planets last year? Mr. Marrs can't be a Martian. There's no life on Mars."

I was twirling a piece of popcorn on the table and being careful to keep my eyes down so I wouldn't look foolish. "I don't know about that. The evidence is stacking up that he really is from Mars. I've been doing research."

When I looked up, Sharon, Nicho, and Kelly were staring at me, their mouths hanging open.

"Like what?"

I shrugged. "People spot UFOs all the time. Mr. Marrs is short enough. He could fit inside one."

Kelly flicked her ponytail. "My father says only crackpots see UFOs. Besides, we sent spaceships up to Mars. We know there isn't any life there."

I shook my head no. "Our *Viking* landers were supposed to find out if there was life on Mars by testing the soil. But they only tested the two places where the *Viking* ships landed. Some scientists think that the landers performed the wrong kinds of experiments or looked in the wrong places. A lot of Mars is unexplored. It's also possible that the Martians left Mars before we got there. They could be searching for a place to land."

"You mean, they're like orphans? That's sad," Sharon said.

I couldn't stop myself. "I don't know about sad but a lot of things are possible," I said. "In some places where the *Vikings* landed, the tests indicated salts might be in the soil. Have you ever noticed how Mr. Marrs keeps taking little handfuls of salt?"

Nicho sat back down, slowly. "Yeah, and what about all the water he drinks?"

Kelly rolled her eyes. "Salt makes you thirsty, dummy."

"Exactly. But there's not much water on Mars. So . . ."

"No water?" Nicho repeated.

I shook my head. "Not like we know it. There is high humidity in the atmosphere, so atmospheric water is available, you know, to a Martian. There are morning fogs, polar hoods, and other water clouds."

"Gosh, Jerry," Kelly interrupted. "You're a walking encyclopedia."

"And another thing," I went on. "Remember when we did our weather skits and Mr. Marrs said he knew a lot about dust storms? Mars has colossal dust storms that sometimes last for weeks. He'd know about dust storms, all right."

With Nicho, Kelly, and Sharon leaning forward and listening to every word I said, it was hard to keep my head from spinning.

"And don't forget Marrs's hair." I was being dramatic. "Did you ever see hair that red before? I bet the iron oxides in the soil make everything red, especially hair."

Just then Kelly reached over and messed up Nicho's hair.

"Hey, cut it out!" Nicho stood up fast. He grabbed Kelly's ponytail.

When Kelly screamed, her popcorn went all over the place.

Sharon brushed off her sleeves. "Come on, you guys. Let's get back to Florida."

By three o'clock, I was having so much fun

splashing around in the Everglades with Sharon and a bunch of alligators that good grades were the furthest thing from my mind. So was Mr. Marrs, when suddenly Nicho said, "What if we went over to his house? I know where he lives. It's that house with the red shutters on Delaney Court. Maybe we'll see something."

"That's spying," I said.

"So? If Marrs really is a Martian, what do you think he's doing here?" Nicho said. He wiped his elbows on a towel. "Look, we can't do much else here anyway. Key West is flooded, and our man-eating alligators keep sinking. I say we hop on our bikes and go over to Marrs's house while Florida is drying out."

Spy on a teacher? No one had to tell me what was going to happen next. I was going to get suspended!

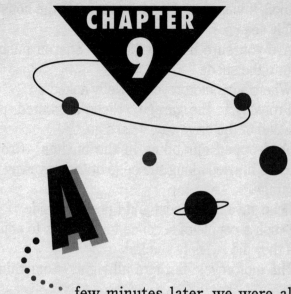

CHAPTER 9

A few minutes later, we were all on our bicycles outside of Sharon's house.

We pushed off. Nicho led the way. Pretty soon, instead of riding in a line, I was cruising alongside of Sharon. Kelly and Nicho were in front.

I tried to keep my mind on pedaling and watching out for pebbles, potholes, and anything that might make me lose my balance. Falling off your bike in front of a girl would not be cool.

The whole time we rode I kept sneaking peeks at Sharon. Once when I noticed she was doing the same thing, my ears got so hot, I almost flew over the handlebars.

Nicho waved us around a corner, then stopped in front of a yard that was overgrown with bushes and shrubs. Since we could barely see the house from where we stood, it was a sure bet no one inside the house could possibly see us.

"Are you sure he lives here?" Sharon pushed her bike into the shade.

"Where's his motorcycle?" Kelly asked.

"Probably in the garage," Nicho answered, pointing to the end of the driveway. "Let's go."

We dropped our bikes in the bushes. Crouching down, we hurried along the edge of the driveway toward the garage.

Nicho gave me a boost and I peeked inside.

It took a couple of seconds for my eyes to adjust, but when they did . . . holy smoke!

"His motorcycle is there all right. Something else, too."

"What?" Sharon whispered back.

"I can't tell. It's under a big sheet." I didn't want to say what I thought it might be.

"Wow. I bet it's his flying saucer."

Secretly, I was glad when Nicho said it instead of me.

Kelly crossed her arms. "A flying saucer? In a garage? Get real. I thought they were supposed to be big."

Sharon looked at me and shrugged. "Maybe it's a private flying saucer."

"And maybe it's not a flying saucer at all," Kelly said, rolling her eyes.

I jumped down.

Nicho started for the house. "Let's go ring his doorbell."

Sharon stepped closer to where I was standing. "I don't think we should. A covered shape in his garage doesn't prove anything. Besides, he'll see us."

"Yeah, right," Nicho said. "Then let's at least peek in his window. C'mon."

"We might as well," Kelly said. "We're already here."

Moving quietly, we slipped into the bushes along the side of his house. As we peered through the window, I found myself standing so close to Sharon I could feel her breath.

"Shhhhhh!"

Except for a brown tweed couch, a broken-down chair, and a television set, the room was practically empty. On the floor in the corner, there was a stack of newspapers beside a telephone. A crimson robe was thrown over the chair.

B-b-b-b-ring.

When the phone rang, I almost flew out of my skin. So did the others. Nicho clamped his hand over Kelly's mouth to keep her from screaming out loud.

Beside me, Sharon gasped as a green creature dashed into the living room to answer the phone. If it wasn't for the white moon boots and the silver helmet, we never would have recognized him.

Yikes!

Mr. Marrs really was a Martian.

CHAPTER
10

A fairy godmother kissed Tony's forehead, then mine. It was Mom in a really cool costume. She was going to a party for teachers. I was in charge of entertaining Tony again.

But before Mom swooped out into the dark night, there were a couple of important things I had to know. Like, "Hey, Mom. Where do teachers come from?"

I already knew how teachers had to go to college to get a degree and a special certificate that said they could teach certain grades.

What I didn't know was that superintendents and principals were supposed to do background checks on teachers to make sure they wouldn't do anything to hurt a kid.

Mom knew our class had gone through more than a few subs. She probably thought she was making me feel better.

Not a chance.

Mom's car had barely pulled out on the street when the phone rang.

"I've got it," Tony screamed into the receiver. Then he dropped it on the floor.

"Ouch!" Nicho said on the other end of the phone. "Okay, so what do we do about Marrs? No one will believe what we saw. It'll come down to his word against ours."

Why hadn't I thought of that before? "His journal!" I yelled. "He writes in it every day. I bet it's loaded with Martian stuff."

"What? Steal his journal from his desk?"

"Not steal—borrow. Just long enough to read it and show it to Dr. Drucker."

Nicho whistled long and low into the phone. "This is major. We're going to need help."

"What about Sharon and Kelly?"

"Good idea. Hey, that reminds me," Nicho said suddenly. "I was talking to Kelly and she says that Sharon says that she likes you. Sharon thinks you're funny. She liked it when you did that tornado thing. And she wasn't even mad when your alligator ate up Key West. You're not supposed to know."

All thoughts of Marrs vanished.

"So, what am I supposed to do?"

"Call her, stupid. Here's her number. I went to a lot of trouble to get it."

I fished a pen out of Mom's kitchen drawer and wrote Sharon's number on the palm of my hand where I wouldn't lose it. Then, just so I wouldn't forget whose number it was, I wrote her name on the outside of my hand and underlined it twice so I'd be sure to call.

"Hey, Tony," I shouted. "How about if we build a fort?"

Tony loves forts. Besides, if I was going to talk to a girl on the telephone, I definitely did not need a little brother hanging around and mimicking every goofball thing I said.

"Cool, Jerry. Can Rusty play in the fort, too?"

"Sure. You and Rusty can even guard the fort while I use the phone to call for reinforcements. C'mon. I'll build you a fort so super you won't ever want to come out!"

It was fun. With Tony's help, I draped blankets, sheets, and bedspreads over tables and chairs until the entire living room was transformed into a maze of tunnels leading from one fort to the next.

Tony lifted the flap I'd created in front of the television and poked his head out. "You can call for reinforcements now, Jerry."

"Okay, scout. If you hear rifles in the distance, don't worry. It'll only be popcorn."

"Don't forget lettuce for Rusty."

While the popcorn exploded in the microwave, I opened a soda and washed a lettuce leaf. Then I carried everything to Tony, who was waiting like a trooper.

Back in the kitchen I took a deep breath and picked up the phone. At the same time, I turned my hand over to read the number.

"Yaaaaaeeeaagh!" The numbers were smeared, probably from washing Rusty's lettuce. It only took me about five tries to get the number right.

Finally . . .

"Hello. Can I speak to Sharon?"

"Just a minute. I'll find her. SHARON!!! It's for you. I THINK IT'S A BOY!"

She *thinks* it's a boy? She couldn't tell? Maybe I should hang up while I still had a chance.

I could hear muffled noises in the background that sounded vaguely like someone getting killed, followed by footsteps and someone picking up the phone.

"Hello?" It was Sharon.

I cleared my throat, hoping it would help. "Hello."

"Jerry. Oh, good!" Sharon breathed a sigh of relief. "I didn't say anything to my parents about what we saw. Did you say anything to your mother?"

"No." I tried to sound calm. "But the superintendent is supposed to do background checks to make sure none of our teachers are criminals. I wonder if he checks out substitutes."

"What are we going to do?" Sharon whispered. "What if Marrs kidnaps somebody? I asked my big sister about Martians and she said they take people for rides in their flying saucers. If the people come back, the only thing they remember is little green men with bulging eyes and bald heads."

"Huh," I said, thinking out loud. "That explains it. Marrs's red hair must be a wig."

"Wait," Sharon said. "What if Kelly and I yanked it

off and Dr. Drucker saw his green, bald head?"

"Hold it," I said quickly. "Nicho and I already have a plan. We're breaking into Marrs's desk after school to get his journal."

"Well, we're not waiting until after school. Kelly and I are going after his wig tomorrow afternoon." And then she said what I'd been hoping to hear. "If we don't get the wig and you still need to break into Marrs's desk, Kelly and I will be your lookouts."

It should have made me breathe a little easier. I wasn't chicken, but I wasn't dumb, either. Secretly I hoped Sharon and Kelly were successful. Breaking into a teacher's desk was serious stuff—even if the teacher was from Mars.

CHAPTER 11

woke up the next morning thinking of Mr. Marrs. I couldn't get him out of my mind. I kept thinking how it was only because of him that Nicho, Kelly, and most of all, Sharon, were my friends. Part of me didn't want to turn Marrs in. It almost felt like I was betraying him.

If only I could believe that Mr. Marrs didn't mean any harm. But how could you be sure about a substitute teacher from Mars?

All morning I felt Mr. Marrs watching me. Knowing that he was probably reading my mind, I covered my head and ducked behind Wilber Robertson. Every time Wilber shifted a quarter inch to the left or right, I shifted, too.

To anyone else, it would appear I was really getting into my schoolwork. Actually, I was busy preparing to save the entire population of Bigelow Springs Elementary, if not the entire planet.

It didn't take long for my shoulders to ache from scrunching like a turtle. My neck didn't feel any better. If I stayed in this position much longer, my bones would warp permanently.

Just then Wilber sneezed. *Ca-floey!*

Uh-oh! Wilber shifted in his chair, putting me in range. When I glanced up, Marrs was beaming in on me. And smiling.

Quickly, I ducked my head.

There was only one thing I could do. I wouldn't think about what I didn't want Mr. Marrs to know. I'd think about someone else.

The problem was, every time I thought of Sharon, my ears burned in the worst way.

"Pssst, Donatelli." Nicho passed me a note folded in the shape of a tiny triangle.

Carefully, I unfolded it. It was from Sharon.

> Dear Jerry,
> What's the matter with your ears?
> They're really red.
> You should go to the clinic. You might
> have an ear infection.
> Kelly and I are going after Marrs's wig.
> Wish us luck.
>
> > Love,
> > Sharon

Love? Now my ears burned more than ever.

Still keeping my head down, I tried signaling to Sharon. What she and Kelly planned was too dangerous.

Sharon raised her hand. "Mr. Marrs, it's awfully hot in here." As if to prove it, she pulled at her T-shirt and blew on her face. "Mrs. Meriweather keeps a fan in the coat closet."

Mr. Marrs tapped his finger on the desk while his eyes swept suspiciously around the room. "Fine, but let's keep the fan on the lowest setting. We don't need test papers blowing into space."

Kelly stood up so fast, her chair scraped the floor. "I'll help."

While the rest of us pretended to be absorbed with our assignment, Sharon and Kelly set the fan on the table beside the teacher's desk.

"Thank you, girls. You can return to your seats now. I'm sure Mrs. Meriweather's fan will bring relief to our heated atmosphere." If Marrs suspected anything, he didn't let on.

You could tell Kelly was stalling. Sharon hadn't budged either. Her eyes were glued on the fan.

Sharon hit the control button.

The sharp gust of air caught Marrs full force. Papers flew everywhere.

"Help! I can't stop it." Sharon grabbed the bottom of the fan. Shutting her eyes, she aimed it right at the substitute's red hair.

Marrs leaped out of his chair. With a hard yank, he pulled the cord out of the wall. "Sharon, are you all right?"

If we didn't know better, we might have thought we had a genuinely concerned substitute teacher.

Sharon blushed. Her dark lashes fluttered. "Um, yes. Maybe I . . . I think . . . I could use . . . a drink . . . of water. May I be excused . . . please?"

Kelly's hand grabbed for the doorknob. "Me, too."

I couldn't stand it any longer. I had to do something. But as I started to get up, Sharon sent me a warning look that said, "Stay where you are or else!"

Quickly, I ducked back behind Wilber's hulking shoulders.

A few minutes later the girls returned to clean up the mess they'd made at Marrs's desk.

"Oooh, gross!" Kelly yelled. "A bug!"

"It's huge! And it's in your hair," Sharon yelled at Marrs. "Don't move, Mr. Marrs!"

Sharon never gave him a chance. Instead, she and Kelly dove at his hair.

"Yeeeouch!"

As Nicho and the rest of us stared in shock, all three of them dropped behind Marrs's desk. When they finally stood up, it was hard to say whose face was the reddest. But one thing was very clear: Marrs's wig was firmly attached. As far as I could tell, it could mean only one thing. Martians had it over us earthlings when it came to glue.

When the bell finally rang for lunch, I followed Wilber. I was determined to keep in Wilber's hulking shadow all the way to the cafeteria.

Like a perfectly coordinated drill team we went up

the aisle, turned a hard right on the toes of our sneakers, and were heading out the door when Marrs called after me.

"Jerry, could I see you for a moment."

Uh-oh.

"I know what you're thinking."

Why was I not surprised? I tried as hard as I could to act natural.

Marrs poked at the mound of plastic dog poop someone had left on his desk. "I want to put your fears to rest."

Gulp! How was he going to do that?

"I've been quite careful with the drawings you did for Spirit Week and the others Mrs. Meriweather had filed in your portfolio."

What?

"Yes. I've taken the liberty of sending some of your artwork to the County Scholarship Committee. The county is sponsoring a summer internship program at the community college. The instructors are professional artists from New York. I think you stand a good chance. In any event, I think you are a tremendously talented young man. You have a rare ability for taking ordinary observations and portraying them with humor and in a startling and refreshing manner that touches your audience. I hope you'll always remember that talent is a special gift. It's your responsibility to use it wisely."

I staggered out of the classroom, totally confused by what Marrs had said. Was that really me Marrs was talking about? Or was Marrs trying to trick me so Nicho and I would cancel our plans?

Nicho was in the hallway waiting. "What was that all about?"

"I'm not sure."

Why did Marrs have to be so clever, I wondered as Nicho and I hurried toward the cafeteria.

Why did some decisions have to be so tough?

CHAPTER
12

he kids were waiting for us in the
cafeteria. Thanks to Kelly, our class was buzzing
about what we'd seen through Marrs's window. But
nobody, except the four of us, knew of my plan to get
Marrs's journal. On that, Sharon made certain Kelly
kept quiet. Now as Nicho and I strode into the
lunchroom, it was my job to fill everyone in.

"You guys, listen to Donatelli." Nicho motioned the
kids to lean closer around the table.

What we were about to do didn't hit me until I saw
their trusting faces. So far we'd done a lot of things to
substitute teachers, but nothing mean or destructive —
unless you counted mental breakdowns. Peeking in a
teacher's window was bad enough. Breaking into a
teacher's desk was serious business.

"I say we don't have a choice," I told them. "Dr.

Drucker won't believe us unless we prove it with Marrs's own words. We've all seen Marrs writing in his journal. That journal has got to be a dead giveaway."

When I said the part about the dead giveaway, Sharon grimaced.

Maybe she was right. Maybe I was over-dramatizing. But when I was saving the whole school from being sued, and maybe preventing a kid from being kidnapped by a Martian, I figured I was entitled.

"Somebody's got to stop Marrs before it's too late." I dropped my voice. "Here's what we do. We meet on the playground after school. When Marrs leaves, we circle back to the building, going in different doors at different times. Teachers get suspicious when a bunch of kids comes *in* to a school."

"What about your brother?" Sharon asked. "Aren't you supposed to walk him home?"

"I already saw to that. He's going home with one of his friends." I turned back to the others. "Okay. Nicho and I will be the ones to break into the desk. I need five more people to go with us." I glanced around the table. "Any volunteers?"

If I hadn't been planning the invasion of the century, I might have smiled when their hands flew up. But I was too nervous. "Great. Freddie, Victor, Paul, Kelly, Sharon."

I swallowed. All I could do now was wait out the rest of the afternoon crouched in Wilber's hulking shadow. It was the longest afternoon of my life. Finally, the bell rang for dismissal.

As planned, we met on the playground. After checking our watches and waiting until it was safe, Sharon and Kelly walked around to the side door. A few minutes later, Freddie and Paul entered through the cafeteria. Nicho strolled casually through the front door. I went next, knowing that Victor would follow.

When we entered our empty classroom, the shades were drawn halfway. The afternoon sun gave everything an eerie reddish-orange glow—not unlike Mars.

"Let's get the desk drawer open and get out of here," Nicho whispered.

Taking a deep breath, I pulled the desk drawer.

It wouldn't budge. I tugged again. Nothing. Not an inch.

"Great! It's locked," I muttered. "You try."

Nicho gave it a hard yank. Nothing.

"Here, use this." Sharon handed me her barrette.

Desperate, I poked the silver tip into the lock and twisted. "I think I got it."

This time, when I tugged, the top drawer ran smoothly on its tracks. Quickly, my eyes inventoried the contents of the drawer. Pens, pencils, a pair of scissors.

And then I saw the journal.

Nicho reached for it, but I grabbed it first.

Not wasting a second, I opened it up. Inside was our proof.

Nicho was hanging over my shoulder. "What the . . . "

I almost screamed. "It's written in code!"

We were so busy flipping through the pages searching for something—anything—written in plain

English that we never heard Dr. Drucker enter the room.

"And precisely what do you think you are doing?"

Sharon practically fell off the desk. Paul stepped back and tripped over the trash can. The trash can rolled across the floor. *Ka-bang, ka-bang, ka-bang.* It was the only thing louder than my beating heart.

We were in trouble. Big-time trouble.

I was still trying to think of something smart to say when Nicho started without me.

"Dr. Drucker, I don't know if you noticed, but some very peculiar things have been happening in our classroom."

Dr. Drucker did not look pleased as he rubbed his chin. He was probably trying to decide if he should call the cops, our parents, or both.

"Yes, this class does have a history of strange events," Dr. Drucker said sarcastically.

Nicho didn't seem to notice. "Dr. Drucker, what we're talking about is *extraterrestrial.*"

"Extra?" Dr. Drucker raised his eyebrows.

"Terrestrial," I answered for him.

Behind me, I could hear Freddie and Victor squirming.

"We're all a little afraid. A lot afraid," I corrected. "We're afraid of what might happen to you and the kids at Bigelow Springs. We wouldn't want any parents to sue you."

"I don't think you need to worry. . . ." Dr. Drucker's head turned slightly, questioning.

"Oh, but we do, Dr. Drucker. I was just getting to that."

"Yeah," Nicho and the others seconded.

"The problem we're having is with Mr. Marrs."

Dr. Drucker looked puzzled. "Oh?"

"It's not a little problem," I said as Nicho nervously scratched his neck. "Mr. Marrs is not exactly what he appears."

"He's not human," Sharon offered.

"I didn't know teachers were supposed to appear human," Dr. Drucker replied. "It might surprise you, but to some adults—and teachers, too, I might add— sixth graders do not appear human. So, I'd say you and Mr. Marrs are probably a pretty good match."

I wasn't exactly sure how to phrase my next question without sounding like a smart-aleck. "Did you do a background check on Mr. Marrs?" I asked as quietly and calmly as I could.

"What is this?" Dr. Drucker sounded angrier than ever. "Who do you think you are, questioning the qualifications of your teachers! Unless you have something terribly earthshaking to say, I won't hear any more of it."

"Earthshaking!" Nicho shouted. "Dr. Drucker, that's exactly what our problem is. This Mr. Marrs guy isn't from anywhere around here."

Sharon stepped bravely forward. "Dr. Drucker, please! Our substitute teacher is from Mars! Jerry can prove it."

Gulp!

Before anyone could say another word, I ran to my desk. I pulled out my binder where I'd recorded the evidence.

"Here!" I shoved my binder under Dr. Drucker's nose. "Read this. Then look at his journal! Mr. Marrs even writes in code! For all we know, he's part of a whole army of Martians. They could be planning a massive invasion."

Dr. Drucker scanned what I'd recorded in my binder. Then he glanced at the code in Mr. Marrs's journal. When he finished, he glared at me with eyes more fearsome than either pair belonging to Marrs—front or back. Dr. Drucker's face grew an angry red. His neck started to swell.

Just when I was about to yell, "Quick, does anybody know CPR?" Dr. Drucker took a deep breath and his face returned to its normal color.

I wasn't about to stop now. "And if Mr. Marrs kidnaps any of us, our parents are going to be really mad. They'll probably sue and you'll have to go to jail." I paused to let what I'd said sunk in. "None of us wants to see you in jail, Dr. Drucker."

Dr. Drucker's left eyebrow raised slightly. "I'll take that under advisement. In the meantime, I'll remind you that a teacher's desk is private property. Breaking into a teacher's desk is unacceptable behavior. Reading a teacher's journal is an invasion of privacy."

Glaring at Nicho and me, Dr. Drucker added, "Some of you are in more trouble than others."

few minutes later Drucker was leaning across his desk and staring at Nicho while talking on the phone to Nicho's dad. "Yes, I realize that, but this is a serious offense and I cannot dismiss your son until you come for him."

I'd never seen Nicho squirm before.

Next Dr. Drucker phoned Sharon's and Kelly's houses. He called my mother at her school, but she was in a meeting. He had the meeting interrupted. "Mrs. Donatelli, this is Principal Drucker. I have Jerry here in the office with me. . . ."

I was dog meat. *Ground* dog meat.

Dr. Drucker hung up the phone and began drumming his fingers on the desk. "You'll need to apologize to Mr. Marrs immediately."

Just then, mind-reading Marrs poked his head in the office.

"I was just about to call you," Dr. Drucker said, sliding Marrs's journal across the desk in my direction. "Jerry. You need to return this to its proper owner. And apologize."

There was no time to think up an excuse.

"Um. We broke into your desk to read your journal. It was my idea and we're sorry," I stammered.

Behind me, Kelly giggled nervously. "We wouldn't have done it except Jerry convinced us that you were a Martian."

Marrs did a double take. "My stars! You didn't tell anyone important, did you?"

Not seeming to notice Marrs's response, Dr. Drucker walked around to the front of his desk. "Perhaps, Mr. Marrs, you can suggest some appropriate discipline."

Marrs studied the bunch of us. "You're in charge here," he finally said to Dr. Drucker. "I'll leave it up to you."

"Well then." Dr. Drucker took a deep breath. "I'll contact you later and let you know what I come up with."

"Fine," Marrs said, tucking his journal safely under his arm before leaving.

"You break-in artists may wait quietly in the hall for your parents," Dr. Drucker said. "I'll see each of you with your parent in private. Until then, no one is to leave."

Silently we took our places on Death Row.

Kelly's mom arrived first, grabbed Kelly by the wrist, and dragged her into Dr. Drucker's office. The office door was still closed when Nicho's father barreled down the hallway. "*Now* what have you done?" he demanded.

"Terrific," Nicho muttered. "There goes my minibike."

When the door opened, Kelly's hands were covering her face as she and her mother left. Nicho and his father headed in.

By now Sharon's mother and the rest of the parents—except for my mom—had arrived. No one looked at anyone else, probably because none of us wanted anyone to know just how scared we were.

When Nicho left, I tried to catch his eye to get a hint of what had happened, but Nicho just kept moving. Victor and his mother went next, followed by Paul and his mother, then Freddie and his father, then Sharon and her mom. Finally, it was just me standing all alone on Death Row.

I ground my toe in the linoleum and waited. I was shaking all over. I was so scared, I didn't hear Mom until she was beside me. "Tell me what happened, Jerry."

Once I started, the words flowed like a river. I was glad that Mom didn't interrupt or tell me what I'd done wrong. She probably figured I'd found that out for myself.

"I didn't mean to let you down," I said.

Mom smoothed my hair with her fingers. "I am disappointed in you, Jerry, but what you did was brave."

"It was?"

Mom nodded. "You truly believed that Mr. Marrs was endangering your friends. It seems to me you made an organized presentation expressing what you believed to be the facts."

"What about breaking into the teacher's desk and taking Mr. Marrs's journal?"

Mom let out a long, tired breath. "That wasn't right. You must have been pretty desperate to prove your case. Next time, how about coming to me first when you have a problem with a teacher?"

I nodded. "Yeah, Mom. I will."

Just then Dr. Drucker signaled for us to come in.

"It was a real bad thing to do," I told Dr. Drucker after we sat down. "And I'm sorry."

"I accept your apology, Jerry, but you realize you have to be punished for this offense. Starting this weekend you and Nicho will spend the next three weekends working on the school grounds. This is in addition to whatever discipline your mother has planned for you. I hope you've learned your lesson."

"Yes, sir. When it comes to discipline, my mom doesn't beat around the bush."

In fact, Mom called Mr. Marrs as soon as we got home. She arranged for me to show up at his house the very next morning to help him with some chores.

I started to remind her how this was probably not a good idea since the evidence still pointed to the fact that he was from Mars and probably had a flying saucer hidden in his garage, but I figured I'd caused enough trouble without bringing that up again.

Instead, early the next morning, I got on my bike and headed down the road. Just as I expected, mind-reading Marrs was waiting in his driveway like he knew exactly when I was coming.

"Greetings! I hope you had a hearty breakfast," Marrs said, pointing to a stack of boxes. "That's my prize collection. Inside you'll find a slew of nuts, bolts, wheels, wires, tubes, fan blades, and whatever. Your job is to clean off the grime and sort everything by category. Here are some rags and de-greaser. I'll be in the garage if you need me."

Ugh. Three boxes of grease, grime, and whatever. By the time I was finished scrubbing, my fingerprints would probably wear off.

I was starting on the second box when Marrs came over and spoke to me.

"What happened yesterday after I left? Did Dr. Drucker decide on a punishment?"

"We have to do a bunch of yard work around the school." I dipped a rag into the cleaning goo and began rubbing the outside dome of a peculiar-looking light fixture. "Dr. Drucker says Nicho and I are now head of his Daffodil Brigade. It's going to keep us busy for the rest of the month."

"Sounds fair."

"Yeah. We deserved it all right. We never should have broken into your desk. We're really sorry about that, Mr. Marrs."

"I know you are, Jerry," Marrs said, picking up a rag and another odd piece of metal. "You guys are what teaching is all about."

"Well, as a matter of fact, we were trying to get into the *Guinness Book of World Records.*"

"Oh?"

"Yeah, for having the most substitute teachers in a year. The problem was, you were a good teacher and you kept coming back! And then instead of getting into the record books we wound up in a bunch of trouble."

Marrs tossed a couple of bolts in the pile I'd built up in the grass. "You might still make history. I'm sure there's another avenue smart kids like you . . ."

I wasn't listening.

"This is crazy." I turned the peculiar light dome over in my hand. "I've seen this thing before. Where? What is this?" I asked. "What's it for?"

Grinning, Marrs removed whatever it was from my hand. "I'd show you, but we're running out of time and we don't want your mother to worry. But, Jerry, you're clever. Why don't you just . . ."

Putting his thumb on his forehead and wiggling his four fingers, Marrs added, "Think on it."

CHAPTER
14

was still "thinking on it" Monday morning when I walked into our classroom and practically bumped into our regular teacher, Mrs. Meriweather.

"Whoa, Jerry!"

"What happened to Mr. Marrs?" I blurted.

"Nothing." Mrs. Meriweather smiled. "It's just that I'm back."

For the rest of the day, we brought Mrs. Meriweather up to date on our schoolwork and projects. I could tell she was surprised that I had worked on Florida with Sharon, Kelly, and Nicho. She didn't exactly give us an A for Florida, but she didn't give us an F either.

Later, Mrs. Meriweather told me that Mr. Marrs really *had* sent my drawings into the Scholarship

Committee. She said she never knew about the internship program and if Mr. Marrs hadn't been in the right place at the right time, I never would have had the opportunity. I should thank my lucky stars. Strange that she would use those exact words.

That afternoon, I got on my bike and rode over to Mr. Marrs's house. When I'd looked in my binder after lunch, it dawned on me what was in those cardboard boxes. I also knew where I'd seen that peculiar dome light before—it was the blinking light in my drawing of the spaceship. I wanted to tell Mr. Marrs that his secret was safe with me.

I also wanted to thank Marrs for submitting my drawings to the contest. Maybe he would tell me how he did some of those weird things in our classroom or why he never once lost his temper.

I thought he might even tell me where he *really* came from. Maybe it wasn't an alien place after all. And what had he said about us in his journal? Did he like our sixth-grade class?

Mostly, I wanted to say good-bye.

But when I got over to his house and peeked in the window, his garage was empty.

There was no motorcycle. There was no strange shape covered with a sheet. Even the cardboard boxes were gone. There was only a broom with a little pile of dust swept into a corner.

I rang the doorbell a couple of times, but there was no answer. When I peeked in the window, the house was empty.

I know it sounds stupid, but I was thinking maybe he'd just gone to the store. Maybe he really hadn't pulled up and left like that. Maybe he was standing next to the lobster tank with one of Nicho's rubber worms. I mean, maybe he hadn't really meant to leave without saying good-bye.

Maybe he didn't have a choice. Maybe it was a Martian emergency.

The following Saturday, Nicho and I were working our fingers to the bone for the Drucker Daffodil Brigade. By two o'clock, we'd dumped mulch around all of Dr. Drucker's droopy daffodils. We'd weeded out miles of flower beds and picked up the trash stupid high school kids threw in the bushes by the road. We'd edged the sidewalk by the driveway and pulled up about half a million weeds.

I was wiping the sweat off my forehead with the side of my arm when Kelly and Sharon walked up.

"You guys," Kelly called out.

Sharon picked up a rake and began easing chunks of pine bark through the tiny blades of grass and back around the daffodils where they belonged. "It's not fair. You guys got a bigger punishment than the rest of us."

I shrugged.

"Anyway, that was really dumb of you to think Mr. Marrs was a Martian," Kelly said.

Nicho stopped picking up trash. "Why don't you tell her?" he asked me.

Kelly hit Nicho's arm. "Tell me what?"

Nicho dropped the trash bag and yelled, "Marrs moved out!"

"So?"

Nicho shook his head in disbelief. "So, it's like Donatelli said. Martians always zip in and out before people discover who they are. Don't you think it's kind of suspicious? Marrs vanished the minute we were on to him."

Kelly crossed her arms. "I think you're nuts. Anyway, we didn't come over here to talk about stupid Martian junk. Sharon is having a party next Saturday. She needs a special theme."

Sharon blushed. "Like Hawaii or . . ." She pushed her hair over her shoulder. "Jerry, you dream up the best ideas. Can you think of something boys and girls will like? It's my first boy-girl party. And you better be there. Both of you."

"Promise you won't laugh."

It was Saturday night. Tony was upstairs giving his turtle a bath, so it was just Mom and me in the family room.

"You have to promise not to bite the side of your mouth. You have to promise not to make your eyes twinkle."

Mom grabbed me around the waist so fast she knocked the baseball cap off my head. "Jerry!"

I wiggled free and set the baseball cap back on my head where it belonged.

Mom leaned back on the couch and stared up at the ceiling. "Okay. I will promise not to laugh. I will promise anything I can reasonably expect myself not to do. But, Jerry, I can't promise not to twinkle."

She turned around sideways, bringing her leg up

under her, and stared at me. "Besides, what could possibly be so embarrassingly funny?"

Now I felt foolish. "It's not funny."

"Embarrassing then."

I shrugged. "Maybe it's not even embarrassing."

Mom's eyes were starting to twinkle. "Then why?"

"Mom!"

"What?"

"Your eyes."

"They are not twinkling, Jerry. Now are you going to tell me, or am I going to have to . . ."

This time when she lunged, I moved faster. I sat down in Dad's old chair and folded my arms across my chest. I put my ankle on my knee and tried to look like the way I remembered Dad.

I was watching Mom very closely. If she started to smile, if she started biting the side of her mouth, if her eyes twinkled more than they usually do, then I was going to stop.

"Okay." I took a deep breath. "Sharon invited me and Nicho to her party. She wants me to think of some things to do. And that's the problem, Mom. What am I supposed to do at a party? It's not just guys. It's guys *and* girls."

Mom cleared her throat. I had to give her credit. She was doing a good job of not doing any of those things she'd promised not to do.

"Well, at the party I went to last week, everyone came dressed in costumes. We stood around, talked, told jokes, and ate meatballs. It was fun."

"Meatballs and jokes are okay."

Mom went on. "Of course, that party was for adults. From what I hear from the kids I teach, what usually happens is the boys go to one side of the room and the girls go to another until some girl gets the bright idea that somebody should play games or dance or . . ."

"Dance? Yuck!"

I grabbed my sides. I dropped to the floor and rolled until I was on my back. Then I kicked my legs and waved my arms like a dead bug. "Maybe I could get sick. Maybe I could die. Maybe I could . . ."

Mom was staring at me like I'd gone bonkers. "Jerry, I've seen you dancing in front of the mirror in your room. You look exactly like a tornado whirling around. A very handsome tornado."

I got up off the floor and went back to sitting on the couch next to Mom. "Sharon wants me to think of a theme. According to her, I always come up with good ideas."

Mom nodded. "That's true. You are one of the most creative people I know."

I was staring at my toes. "That's what she said."

"Bright girl. She might even like you."

"Mom! You're not supposed to say that. This is awful. I used to feel pressure for getting good grades. Girls are worse than grades. With grades, you study a book. But with girls, my ears burn up."

Mom patted my knee. "Sounds like you're maturing. You know, when you were sitting across the room in that chair a few minutes ago, you reminded me of your father.

Jerry, he would be so very proud of you."

Huh? "Do you really think Dad would have been proud of me?"

"I know he would."

Talking to Mom like that made me feel very grown-up. I took my baseball cap off and set it on the table.

"Mr. Marrs said I had a good sense of humor. It would be neat if I could win that art scholarship."

But even as I rattled on about the program at the community college, ideas for Sharon's party formed in the back of my mind.

If we dressed up in costumes, would the girls forget about dancing and settle for meatballs instead? Maybe I could go as a substitute teacher from Mars.

I started to tell Mom my plan but then the phone rang. It was Gram. Tony came out of the bathroom with Rusty wrapped up a towel. He wanted to tell Gram how well Rusty could swim.

When I heard Mom yakking away about how I had made a whole bunch of new friends and was going to my first boy-girl party, I snuck up the stairs.

No way was I talking to Gram tonight.

I waited to call Sharon until after I took my shower. I rehearsed what I would say while I combed my hair in the mirror.

"Hello. This is Jerry. May I speak to Sharon?"

Dialing Sharon's number was not so hard this time. It only took three tries. With practice, I might get it right by next week.

Sharon answered the phone on the first ring. I don't think she was exactly sitting there waiting for me to call, but she was close by. Secretly, I was relieved not to have to talk to her sister—or her mom.

When I told Sharon my idea, she was pretty excited. She put Nicho and me in charge of making sure that the guys wore neat costumes. Sharon didn't want a bunch of bums coming to her party.

I didn't tell her what I was going to be. You know me. I'm full of surprises!

After we hung up, I went to our basement. Mom was reading a book to Tony when I walked past carrying my telescope. She didn't say a word.

My telescope had been in the basement ever since we moved. My dad and I used to look at the stars a lot. But it's only recently that I remembered the telescope was there.

One thing about a telescope, unless you are talking about one of those super-duper observatory kinds of telescopes that sit on mountaintops, you really need to be outside to see anything. Looking through a bedroom window doesn't work well, especially when your mom is too busy teaching kids about Shakespeare to wash the windows.

I unlocked my window, pushing the top half down.

For a moment, all I could do was stand there as the night air chilled my skin. There wasn't a sound.

I stepped back and positioned my telescope until the scope was outside my window. I put my eye to the lens and focused slowly until the universe exploded before my eye.

I didn't bother with the planets or stars. Instead, I searched the black space for a sign—a blinking light, a flash or a flicker. Anything.

Are you out there, Mr. Marrs?